To:

From:

This book belongs to:

_____

GOD GIVES STRENGTH

Dedicated to my sons Terry and Rye. I pray that you grow in God's strength & keep adventuring together. I love you bigger than the world. ♡

ISAIAH 40:29-31

GOD GIVES STRENGTH

By Melissa Wingo

One day, not so long ago.....

Rye asked,
"Terry, what are we
going to do today?".

Terry answered,
"I don't know."

HE GIVES POWER TO THE FAINT

...but then...

Terry jumps up and says,
"I've got a great idea!"

AND TO HIM WHO HAS NO MIGHT

Rye asks, "What is it?"

and Terry says, "Let's build a fort."

HE INCREASES STRENGTH

So Rye grabs his gear and Terry is ready too.

EVEN YOUTHS SHALL

They head outside.

FAINT AND Be weary

First, they gather
their materials.

Push,
Pull,
Drag....

AND YOUNG MEN SHALL FALL EXHAUSTED;

They hammer and dig and
get a little tired.

BUT THEY WHO WAIT FOR THE LORD

So they take a work break.

SHALL RENEW
THEIR STRENGTH

THEY SHALL MOUNT UP WITH WINGS

"Let's build! says Terry.
Bang, Bang
Clunk, Clunk
Clang, Clang

LIKE EAGLES

Finally, it is all done!!

Terry yells, "Look out below."

"Ha, you missed me!"
Rye yells back.

AND NOT BE WEARY!

Terry says, "I like our fort".
Rye says, "I like it too."

THEY SHALL WALK

Then they hear their mom calling them home.

Dinner Time
Dinner Time
Dinner Time

AND NOT FAINT.

...and a warm dinner is waiting for them at the table.

ISAIAH 40:29-31

Their dad asks, "What did you boys do today?"

Both boys look at each other and answer, "....Oh, not too much...."

THE
END

ISAIAH 40:29-31

My name is Melissa Wingo and I am a author/illustrator of Children's books. I live in Sunny California with my husband and three kids. I love books, drawing, the Bible, gardening and running.

THANK YOU

Made in United States
North Haven, CT
17 April 2023

35551508R00024